For Sinéad
N.P.

For Sarah Haddon Furness
I.B.

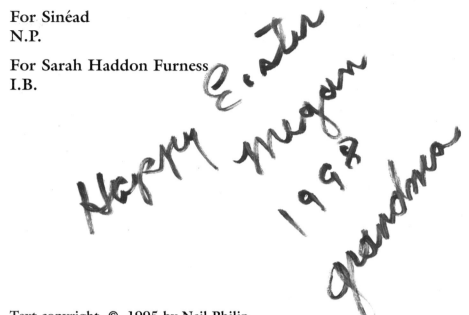

First U.S. edition

ISBN 0-316-70522-5

Library of Congress Catalog Card Number 95-79578

10 9 8 7 6 5 4 3 2 1

Conceived, designed, and produced by The Albion Press Ltd.,
Spring Hill, Idbury, Oxfordshire OX7 6RU, England

Published simultaneously in Canada by
Little, Brown & Company (Canada) Limited and
in Great Britain by Little, Brown and Company (UK)

Printed in Italy

THE GOLDEN BIRD

Retold from the Brothers Grimm by
Neil Philip

Illustrated by
Isabelle Brent

Little, Brown and Company
Boston   New York   Toronto   London

Long, long ago, there was a king whose greatest treasure was a tree that bore golden apples. Every morning, the king went into his pleasure garden to count the apples.

One morning, to his horror, the king discovered that one of the apples was missing.

The king called his eldest son and told him, "Tonight you must stand guard beneath the tree and catch the thief." But that night, the eldest son couldn't keep his eyes open, and in the morning, another golden apple was gone.

Furious, the king summoned his middle son and told him to guard the tree. But the same thing happened. The middle son fell asleep, and in the morning a third apple was gone.

Then it was the turn of the youngest son.

Now, the first two sons were roaring boys, full of swagger and swank, but the youngest son was a quiet lad. So while the king thought the first two were proper princes, and a credit to him, he hadn't much time for the youngest. "I don't suppose you'll be much help," he said, "but since your brothers failed, I might as well give you a try."

At midnight, the youngest son, like his brothers before him, felt his eyelids growing heavy. But he shook himself awake, determined to catch the daring thief who was stealing the king's precious golden apples.

On the last stroke of midnight, he heard a rustling in the air. Looking up, he saw a bird, its feathers glistening in the moonlight. As the bird seized an apple, the young prince drew back his bow and sent an arrow whistling through the air.

The bird flew off, but the arrow had grazed it. One single perfect golden feather fluttered to the ground.

When his son showed him the golden feather, the king said, "This is worth more than my whole kingdom." He turned to the youngest son and snapped, "You fool. Your brothers would never have missed. One feather is not enough. I must, and I will, have the whole bird."

So the king sent his eldest son out to search for the golden bird.

The eldest son came to the edge of a wood, where he saw a fox. He drew his bow, but the fox called out, "Don't shoot! For I can tell you how to find the golden bird."

But the prince just sneered, saying, "I can find the bird by myself, without the help of vermin."

"Listen to me," pleaded the fox. "When you come to the village, enter the down-at-heel inn, not the brightly lit one. They will enchant you there, and you will never be free again."

In reply, the prince fired an arrow at the fox, but the animal whisked away to safety.

That night, the eldest prince came to a village, where, as the fox had said, there were two inns. One was all shabby and dark, while the other was well kept and well lighted; from within welled the merry sounds of laughter and music. The prince opened its door and entered. . . .

Months passed, and the eldest prince did not return. So the second prince set out after him. He, too, met the fox but would not listen to its advice. He, too, came to the village with the two inns, and there he found his brother. "Come and join us!" called the eldest prince, and the middle brother did.

At last, when neither of his trusted sons returned — for they had forgotten their quest while under enchantment — the king sent his youngest son out in search of the golden bird. "At least try not to get lost," he said.

When the youngest son reached the wood, he put down his bow and listened to the fox's advice.

"If you wish to find the golden bird," said the fox, "I will help you. When you reach the village, do not enter the brightly lit inn. Spend the night in the humble one."

The youngest son did as he was told, and after a night of rest and quiet, he set out once more in search of the golden bird. On the road, he again met the fox.

"At the end of this road," said the fox, "you will come to a castle, with a whole company of soldiers slumbering and snoring outside its walls. Don't worry about them, but go right into the castle and through all its rooms. In the very last room, you'll find the golden bird, hanging in a simple wooden cage. Beside it will be a splendid golden cage, but leave that one alone and take the simple one."

The prince did as the fox told him, but when he saw the magnificent golden cage, he couldn't resist it. "This is more fitting for such a beautiful bird," he said.

He opened the wooden cage, but as soon as he touched the golden bird, it screeched out in alarm.

The soldiers awoke and promptly flung the young prince into prison.

The next day, he was taken to the powerful magician who owned the golden bird and was sentenced to death as a thief.

"But," said the magician, "I will let you off, and even give you the golden bird as a reward, if you can bring me the golden horse that runs faster than the wind."

The young prince set off, sighing and sad. How was he to find the golden horse? But on the road, he met his friend the fox.

"This would never have happened if you had listened to me," said the fox. "However, I will help you. At the end of this road, you will come to another castle. Outside the stables, you will see a gang of stable lads snoozing and snoring. Don't worry about them, but go straight in, and in the farthest stable, you will find the horse. Saddle it with the old worn leather saddle, not the golden one that hangs beside it, and all will be well."

The prince followed the fox's instructions, but when it came to saddling the horse, he couldn't bear to shame the golden steed by putting on the old, plain saddle. "Such a magnificent creature deserves the best," he said.

As soon as the gold saddle touched the horse, it began to neigh loudly, waking the grooms, who dragged the prince off to prison.

The next morning, the king of this castle sentenced him to death but said, "I will let you off, and even give you the golden horse as a reward, if you can bring me the beautiful princess from the golden castle."

The young prince set out once more, sighing and sad. But his heart lifted when along the way, he met his old friend the fox.

"You've brought this trouble on yourself," said the fox, "by ignoring my advice. But I feel sorry for you, so I will help you yet again. At the end of this road, you will find the golden castle. Every evening when all is quiet, the beautiful princess goes out to the bathhouse to bathe. As she goes in, run up to her and give her a kiss. She will follow you, and you can take her away with you. But don't let her say good-bye to her parents, or you'll regret it."

Everything went as the fox had said, and the princess said she would be happy to go with the prince. But she begged and pleaded to be allowed to say good-bye to her parents, and when she fell on her knees at his feet, the prince could not deny her.

As soon as the princess reached her father's bedside, he awoke, and the rest of the castle with him, and the young prince was once more flung into prison.

The king said, "You shall die for this. But I will let you go, and take the beautiful princess with you, if you remove the mountain that blocks the view from my window. You have eight days to do it."

For seven days, the young prince dug away, but all his efforts were in vain. That evening, the fox appeared and said, "This is all your own fault, but since you were kind to me, I'll help you once more. Go to sleep, and I will move the mountain." So the prince went off to sleep. When he awoke, the mountain was gone.

He ran to the king, claimed the princess, and set out with her back down the road. There they met the fox, who said, "You have done well, but you can do better still. Take the princess to the king who sent you for her, and he will give you the golden horse in return. Mount it, swing the princess up behind you and gallop away, faster than the wind. No one will be able to catch you."

The trick worked. Then the fox said, "Next you must get the golden bird. When you ride into the castle, they will bring it. Seize the cage and gallop away, faster than the wind."

Soon the prince had all three treasures to take home to his father. The fox said, "Now you can give me my reward."

"What do you desire?" asked the prince.

"When we get to the wood, shoot me and chop off my head and paws," replied the fox.

But the kindhearted young prince could not bring himself to hurt his friend.

So the fox said, "If you won't kill me, I must leave you. But first I will give you some more advice. Do not buy any gallows meat, and do not sit on the edge of a well."

"That is easy advice to take," said the prince.

So they parted, and the prince and the princess rode on the golden horse till they reached the village with the two inns.

The whole village was in uproar, and when the prince asked what was happening, he was told, "We're going to hang two spendthrift good-for-nothings who've been causing trouble in our village for months." The young prince looked up at the gallows and saw his two brothers standing there.

"Would you set them free?" he asked.

"If someone would pay their debts, we would," the villagers replied. "But who would waste a penny on those rapscallions?" Forgetting the fox's warning, the young prince didn't hesitate and ransomed his two brothers with all the cash he had.

Seeing how rich the young prince had become, the two ungrateful brothers schemed together. When they had all arrived at the wood, the brothers said, "Let's sit in the cool by this well and have a bite to eat." And when the young prince sat down on the rim of the well, they pushed him in.

The two brothers took the bird, the horse, and the princess to their father the king.

"Look what we have brought you," they crowed.

"Well done, boys," said the king, "I am proud of you." But though he was pleased with the gifts, he got little joy from them, for the bird would not sing, the horse would not eat, and the beautiful princess would not smile.

Meanwhile the young prince was lying trapped at the bottom of the well. At last the fox came by and pulled him up by its tail. The fox told him, "Your brothers have sent men to watch the wood and they will kill you if you come out." So the prince dressed himself in beggar's rags as a disguise.

When he arrived at the king's palace, no one knew him, but the bird began to sing, the horse began to eat, and the princess started smiling. She said, "I was feeling so sad, and now my heart has lifted, as if my true love has come." And she told the king about the wicked brothers and their deeds.

Angered, the king ordered everyone in the castle to be brought before him. He did not recognize his youngest son in his rags, but the princess did. She flung her arms around his neck and kissed him.

And so they were married, and the two elder princes were banished forever.

But what became of the poor fox?

One day, much later, the prince went walking again in the wood, and there he met the fox once more. The fox pleaded with him, "You have everything your heart desires, but I am as wretched and miserable as ever. It is in your power to free me, if you will do as I asked before. Shoot me, and chop off my head and paws."

This time, the prince did as the fox asked.

No sooner had he done it than the fox changed into a handsome prince. He was the brother of the beautiful princess, freed at long last from the magic spell that had turned him into a fox.

And then they all lived in happiness to the end of their days.